The Lighthouse Keeper's Favourite Stories

Ronda and David Armitage

The Lighthouse Keeper's Lunch
The Lighthouse Keeper's Picnic
The Lighthouse Keeper's Cat

SCHOLASTIC
PRESS

Scholastic Children's Books,
Commonwealth House, 1-19 New Oxford Street,
London WC1A 1NU, UK
a division of Scholastic Ltd

London ~ New York ~ Toronto ~ Sydney ~ Auckland
Mexico City ~ New Delhi ~ Hong Kong

The Lighthouse Keeper's Lunch was first
published in 1977 by André Deutsch Ltd
Text copyright © Ronda Armitage, 1977
Illustrations copyright © David Armitage, 1977

The Lighthouse Keeper's Picnic was first
published in 1993 by Scholastic Ltd
Text copyright © Ronda Armitage, 1993
Illustrations copyright © David Armitage, 1993

The Lighthouse Keeper's Cat was first
published in 1995 by Scholastic Ltd
Text copyright © Ronda Armitage, 1995
Illustrations copyright © David Armitage, 1995

This omnibus edition first published by Scholastic Ltd, 1999

ISBN 0 590 63746 0

Printed in China

The Lighthouse Keeper's Lunch

Once there was a lighthouse keeper called Mr Grinling. At night time he lived in a small white cottage perched high on the cliffs. In the day time he rowed out to his lighthouse on the rocks to clean and polish the light.

Mr Grinling was a most industrious lighthouse keeper. Come rain . . .

. . . or shine he tended his light.

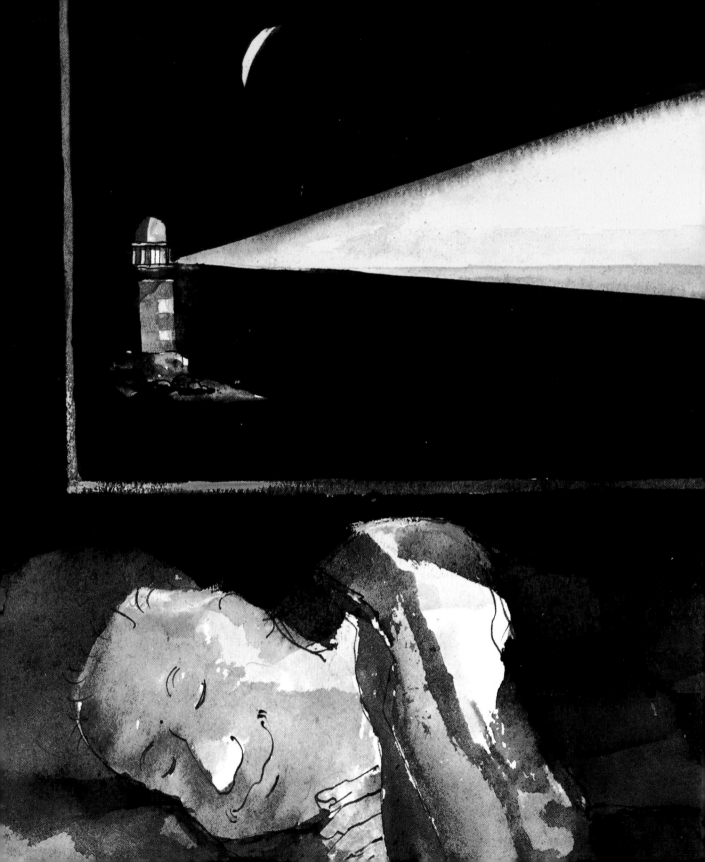

Sometimes at night, as Mr Grinling lay sleeping in his warm bed, the ships would toot to tell him that his light was shining brightly and clearly out to sea.

Each morning while Mr Grinling polished the light Mrs Grinling worked in the kitchen of the little white cottage on the cliffs concocting a delicious lunch for him.

Once she had prepared the lunch she packed it into a special basket and clipped it on to the wire that ran from the little white cottage to the lighthouse on the rocks.

But one Monday something terrible happened. Mrs Grinling had prepared a particularly appetising lunch. She had made . . .

A Mixed Seafood Salad

A Lighthouse Sandwich

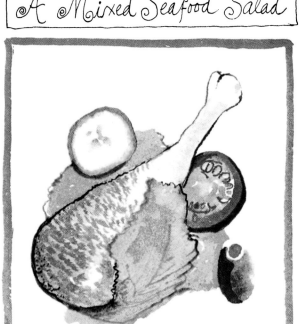

Cold Chicken Garni

2 Sausages and Crisps

Peach Surprise

Iced Sea Biscuits

Drinks and Assorted Fruit

She put the lunch in the basket
as usual and sent it down the wire.

But the lunch did not arrive. It was spotted by three scavenging seagulls who set upon it and devoured it with great gusto.

"Clear off, you varmints," shouted Mr Grinling, but the seagulls took not the slightest notice.

That evening Mr and Mrs Grinling decided on a plan to baffle the seagulls. "Tomorrow I shall tie the napkin to the basket," said Mrs Grinling. "Of course, my dear," agreed Mr Grinling, "a sound plan."

On Tuesday evening Mr and Mrs Grinling racked their
brains for another plan.
"They are a brazen lot, those seagulls," said Mrs Grinling.
"Brazen indeed," said Mr Grinling, "what shall we do?"
"Our cat does not appear to like seagulls," said Mrs Grinling.
"No, my dear," said Mr Grinling, "Hamish is an accomplished
seagull chaser."
"Of course," exclaimed Mrs Grinling, "tomorrow Hamish
can guard the lunch."
"A most ingenious plan," agreed Mr Grinling.

Hamish did not think that this plan was ingenious at all. He spat and hissed as Mrs Grinling secured him in the basket. "There, there, Hamish," said Mrs Grinling consolingly, "I'll have a tasty piece of herring waiting for you when you arrive home."

Sadly, flying did not agree with Hamish. His fur stood on end when the basket swayed, his whiskers drooped when he peered down at the wet, blue sea and he felt much too sick even to notice the seagulls, let alone scare them away from the lunch.

"Lackaday, lackaday,"
said Mr Grinling sadly.
"Miaow, miaow,"
agreed Hamish pitifully.

On Wednesday evening Mr and Mrs Grinling racked their brains again for a new plan. "What shall we do?" said Mr Grinling. Mrs Grinling looked thoughtful. "I have it!" she exclaimed, "just the mixture for hungry seagulls."

"Indeed, my dear," said Mr Grinling, "what have you in mind?" "Wait and see," said Mrs Grinling, "just wait and see."

"Mustard sandwiches," chuckled Mr Grinling.
"A truly superb plan, my dear, truly superb."

On Thursday morning
Mrs Grinling carefully
packed the mustard
sandwiches and sent them
off down the wire to the
expectant seagulls.

On Friday Mrs Grinling repeated the mustard mixture.

So, on Saturday, up in the little white cottage on the cliffs, a jubilant Mrs Grinling put away the mustard pot before she prepared a scrumptious lunch for Mr Grinling.

While he waited for his lunch down in the lighthouse on the rocks,
Mr Grinling sang snatches of old sea shanties as he surveyed the
coastline through his telescope . . .

"Ah well, such is life," mused Mr Grinling as he sat down to enjoy a leisurely lunch in the warm sunshine.

The Lighthouse Keeper's Picnic

Mr Grinling was a lighthouse keeper. He lived with his wife Mrs Grinling and their cat Hamish in a little white cottage on the cliffs. When he was a younger man Mr Grinling used to row out to the lighthouse every morning to clean and polish the light. Now he had an assistant called Sam. Some days Mr Grinling was the lighthouse keeper and some days it was Sam.

On his days off there were lots of things Mr Grinling liked to do.
He liked playing hide and seek with Hamish, he liked growing
geraniums and heliotropes, he liked singing loudly in the village
choir but, most of all, he liked eating. Breakfast, lunch and dinner
and a few little snacks in between. Eating was what he did best.
Sometimes while he ate he would hum a little tune.

Mrs Grinling worried about the eating. "Mr G, don't you think perhaps you're just a bit too rotund?" she asked. "I don't know how you're going to run races at the village picnic tomorrow."
Mr Grinling gazed at himself in the mirror. "Nonsense, Mrs G," he said as he did up his shirt. But he went outside to practise his running before dinner.

Mr Grinling loved the village picnic. All the villagers
came. Big ones and little ones, running and skipping,
huffing and puffing. Mrs Grinling always prepared
a splendid picnic spread and she always kept it as
a surprise.

The picnic day started badly for the Grinlings. They woke up at 9 o'clock instead of 8 o'clock. In the rush Mr Grinling tripped over Hamish. Hamish hid behind the sofa.

They were half way across the bay before they remembered

he was still at home

and half way across again when they remembered

the second lunch basket.

They were very late for the picnic and they forgot to tie up the dinghy.

Everybody was lining up for the egg and spoon race when they arrived. Mr Grinling ran as fast as he was able but he still came last.

He and Joe Jenkins tripped over each other in the three-legged race.

As for the last race he couldn't even fit into the sack, let alone jump.

Mr Grinling was very upset. He stomped off to swim by
himself before lunch. He lay on his back with his tummy in the
air. Up above a rainbow balloon drifted. Mr Grinling sighed.
That would be the life, floating just like a cloud, that's what
he'd really like to do. He sang a floating song to himself:

High in the sky
Gently cruising
Wrapped up in cotton wool
Quietly musing
Singing a cloud song

The picnic lunches were magnificent. Mr Grinling wandered about tasting – a little bit here, a little bit there. But he stopped quite still when he saw Mrs Grinling's spread.

Naughty Nibbles

Bumper Bites

Tempting Treats for Tinies

Melon Boat

Limpet Log

Lighthouse Cake

Salad Crab

Great Green Whale Jelly

Cream Whorls

Starfish Sandwiches

Scallop Sausages

Sea Food

"Sea food" she had called it and it was beautiful. Mr Grinling ate a
piece of everything. "Delicious and delectable," he announced with
his mouth full of green whale jelly. "The best cook here today,
Mrs G, possibly the best cook in the whole, wide world."

Once the picnic was eaten everyone was too full to run or jump any more. Most of the villagers packed up their baskets, and went happily home. Mr and Mrs Grinling felt like a rest. They lay in the sun with their heads under their hats and quietly snored.

When they awoke the sun was beginning to fade, the tide was coming in and the dinghy had floated away.
"Well, that's that," said Mrs Grinling,
"we'll just have to walk home."
Mr Grinling groaned.

They set off around the rocks. In and out, up and down
they went, over and under, rock after rock. Soon the sun
had disappeared. The water came closer. "We must hurry,
Mr G," said Mrs Grinling, "the tide is racing in."

But Mr Grinling couldn't hurry. "I can't climb any more," he puffed, "and I certainly can't climb through that hole, I'll get stuck." Mrs Grinling looked at the hole and she looked at Mr Grinling's tummy. "In that case there's nothing for it," she said, "we'll have to stay here till morning."

They found a flat rock and huddled together to keep warm. The moon came up. The water rose. Once a wave splashed their feet a little but it was only once and then the water began to go down.

Sam was surprised to see the lighthouse light still shining next
morning. When he saw the dinghy nudging against the jetty below
he guessed what had happened. He gazed round the bay.
Yes, there they were; jumping up and down and waving.
He set off right away to rescue them.

Mrs Grinling was cross. Mr Grinling didn't think he'd ever seen her quite so cross. "Mr Grinling," she glared, "that was the coldest and most frightening night I have ever had and all because you're so fat!" Mr Grinling sighed, "You're quite right, Mrs G, I am too fat. What shall I do?"

"Well," said Mrs Grinling, "the cakes will have to go AND the chocolates, the crisps and the sweets." Mr Grinling was horrified, all his favourite foods.

He worked very hard
at getting thinner.

He ran up and down
the path from the
little white cottage
to the dinghy.

He cycled like the wind
into the village
and home again.

Some nights he was so tired
that he fell asleep
in his dinner.

But he did miss the little snacks. "Just one
chocolate biscuit, Mrs G?" he pleaded.
"No, Mr G," she said firmly.
"Not even half of one."

Sam didn't like it when
Mr Grinling was unhappy.
"I'll get you a little
something," he whispered,
"Mrs Grinling need
never know."

Mr Grinling hid the snacks
very carefully, and he ate
only one thing each day.

But when Mrs Grinling told him
to climb on the scales, he was as
heavy as ever. "I don't understand,"
said Mrs Grinling. "You've been so
good, no chocolates or biscuits."
Mr Grinling gazed at the ceiling.

For the next few days Mrs Grinling watched Mr Grinling very closely. She spied from behind the door when he crept into the living room. "Got you, Mr Grinling!" She pounced as his hand reached into the vase. "You should be ashamed of yourself." Mr Grinling hung his head. "Promise me," said Mrs Grinling, "no more snacks." Mr Grinling sighed, "I promise, Mrs G."

Mr Grinling went on trying to get thinner. One day when he was out cycling with Hamish he saw the rainbow balloon again. It was so close he could hear the gentle roar.

"I'd love to float like that," he thought, "as light as a feather. But then I'm not light." He looked at his round tummy. "I don't suppose I'd even fit in the basket," he said gloomily.

He told Mrs Grinling about the balloon that evening.
"Not for you, Mr G," she said, "they'd never get you off the ground."

Mr Grinling got a surprise in the village next day. He saw a large notice in a house window. He knocked at the door.
"I don't suppose I'd be able to have a ride in your balloon?" he asked.

BALLOON RIDES

The balloon lady gazed at him, then slowly she walked round him both ways.
"Of course you can," she said, "and we could probably take Mrs Grinling as well."
Mr Grinling smiled, a great beaming smile.

So that's how the Grinlings went floating one fine afternoon. Hamish and Sam waved them goodbye.

Up over the lighthouse they went and across the bay.
Past the rock where they'd spent that cold night,
over the sea where the whales dived and played,
over the cliffs where the seagulls nested.
And then the land was below, houses and barns
cows, sheep and horses.

Mr Grinling smiled at Mrs Grinling. "This is the best thing
I have ever done," he said. "It's even better than eating."

High in the sky
Gently cruising
Wrapped up in cotton wool
Quietly musing
Singing a cloud song

The
Lighthouse
Keeper's Cat

Hamish lived with Mr and Mrs Grinling
in the little white cottage on the cliffs.
Mr Grinling was the lighthouse keeper.

Some days Hamish went
to work with Mr Grinling.
He liked to help in
the lighthouse.

When visitors came Hamish
would show them round.
"What a magnificent cat!"
they would exclaim.
"Hamish, King of the Lighthouse."

zzzz...

Storm coming
Hamish, let's
go home.

Some days Hamish worked with Mrs Grinling. He liked
digging in the garden where she'd planted the seeds.

He also liked to help with the cooking.
"Fish with everything," was Hamish's motto.
"Not in chocolate cake," said
Mrs Grinling firmly.

A lot of the time Hamish
liked to sleep. One night when
he was curled up in his favourite
place he heard Mr and Mrs
Grinling talking.

Hamish's
Breakfast.

Herbert
Lunch.

HAMISH

PEACH
SURPRISE

"They were there again today," said Mr Grinling, "scampering and squeaking. The Inspector of Lighthouses is coming next week and he says mice might eat the wiring."

"What about Hamish?" asked Mrs Grinling. "He might catch them for you."
Mr Grinling chuckled.
"Our Hamish chase mice? Really, Mrs G, he's much too plump and well fed."
"He might be persuaded if he wasn't quite so well fed," said Mrs Grinling.
"He might chase mice if he didn't have any breakfast before he went to the lighthouse."

"You mean starve him," whispered Mr Grinling.
"Sh, Mrs G, he'll be upset if he hears you."
Hamish was upset, very upset.
"No breakfast," she'd said.
"Starve him," he'd said.

"Well, my quivering ginger whiskers," he thought. "We'll see about that. Nobody starves the lighthouse cat. If they don't love me any more I'll go somewhere else to live."

Early next morning Hamish left home.

As he made his way to the village he met all kinds of strange creatures. Some wanted to chase him and some wanted to play.

He was delighted when he smelt a house.
"Mm, fish," sniffed Hamish, "probably shark."

"Look, Mum," called a little boy,
"there's an enormous cat at our door.
I think he's hungry, can we feed him?"

Hamish liked the breakfast they gave him. He liked the big children. They played hide-and-seek and chase-the-mouse with him.

He didn't like the baby. It rolled on him and squashed his ears.

"Not bad though," thought Hamish
as he jumped up to sleep beside
the stove. "I like this house,
I think I'll stay."

"What's this?" exclaimed the mother.
"A cat who jumps on benches, a
scavenging cat. Not in this house.
Scat cat," she said, "out you go!"

And she shut the door behind him.

"Well, my quivering ginger whiskers,"
thought Hamish, "we'll see about that.
Nobody shouts at this lighthouse cat."

And he stalked off down the road.

A tabby kitten
dropped on him
from a tree.
"Play with me
and you can share
my dinner."

Hamish liked the dinner so much that he forgot to share.

The kitten swung on his tail.
"Play with me and you can sleep in my bed."

Hamish slept in the bed but
he was so large there was
no room for the kitten.

"Who's your ginger friend?"
asked the old man. The kitten
hissed at Hamish. He wasn't
a friend, he didn't share.

But Hamish wanted to stay.
He liked the dinner
and he liked the bed.

"I'll show them how clever I am,"
he thought. "I'll make them
look at me."

But the old man and the
kitten took no notice.
They snored and
purred together.

"Well, my quivering ginger whiskers,"
Hamish glared, "we'll see about that.
Nobody ignores the lighthouse cat."

But he didn't stay grumpy for long. The sun warmed his orange whiskers and the smell of warm mouse tickled his nose.

It was nearly dark when Hamish found the yard. He looked around. "This is no place for a lighthouse cat. Probably mice, possibly rats, maybe . . ."

"CATS!"
They were not pleased to see Hamish.
"Who invited you?" snarled a tattered grey cat.
"This is our place, we don't like strangers," hissed the one-eyed black.
"Skedaddle mush, beat it! You don't belong here."

Hamish skedaddled, right to the top of the tallest tree.

"Well, my quivering ginger whiskers," he puffed,
"We'll see about that. Nobody snarls at the lighthouse cat."

He peered over the branches. The cats' eyes gleamed below.
"Perhaps I'll just stay here for a while," thought Hamish.

The light of the village blinked around him. Far away
another light flashed. Hamish sat up. "My lighthouse!"
He thought about Mr and Mrs Grinling.
He thought about the little white cottage.
The leaves of the trees rustled and the tree began to sway.
"It's time to go home," thought Hamish.

He looked down the tree again. It was too dark to see the
ground any more.

"I don't like going down,"
thought Hamish.
"I CAN'T go down.
I want to go home!"

He yeowled and yeowled but nobody heard him. Then the thunder rumbled and the rain poured down.

He yeowled again, but still nobody heard him. After a while the rain stopped and a soggy, sad, ginger cat went to sleep.

Mrs Grinling heard the thunder too.

"Oh, my poor Hamish," she cried to Mr Grinling. "Where is he? He'll be so frightened."

"There, there, my dear," soothed Mr Grinling. "You know our Hamish, he's a clever cat. He'll be snug and warm or I'll eat my hat."

Next morning Mrs Grinling was up very early. There was no sign of Hamish.

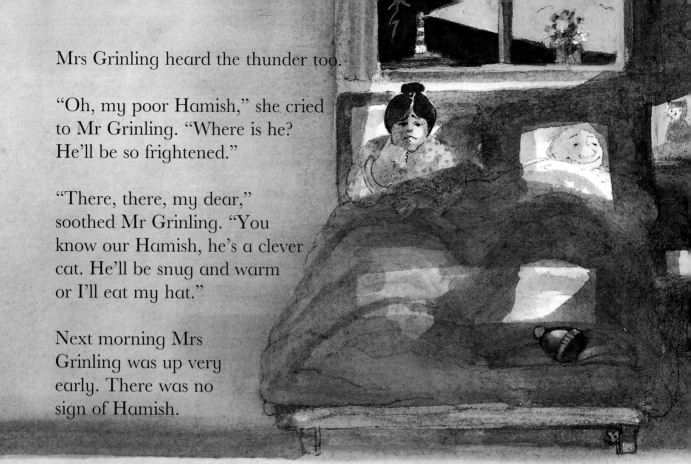

"I'm going out to search for him," she said to Mr Grinling. "He might be hurt."

Before she left she did some cooking. Then she set off for the village on her bike.

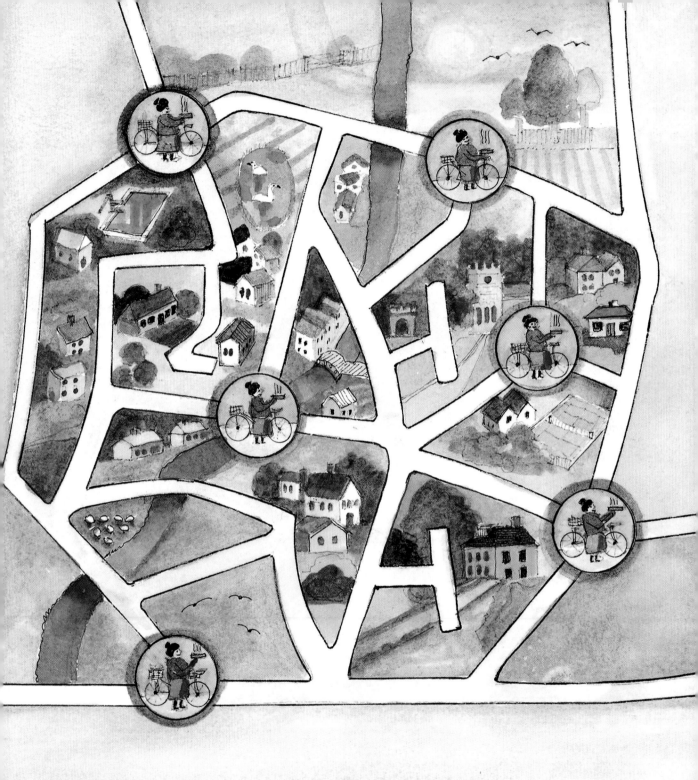

Round and round and up and down she cycled. Every now and then she would stop and take something out of the basket.

Three seagulls arrived at a
very tall tree near the village.
They flew round it, squawking.

"What a caterwauling," exclaimed Mrs Grinling. "What have
they seen in that tree?"

Three seagulls woke
Hamish with their
noise. He meowed.

"Hamish," called Mrs Grinling.
He looked down. His whiskers quivered.
"I know that smell."
His nose nearly fell off his face.

It was his favourite dinner, Star-gazy Pie. Mrs Grinling had cooked it specially. They weren't going to starve him after all.

He meowed and meowed. "You foolish cat," said Mrs Ginling fondly, "I'll come up and get you."

She put the Star-gazy
Pie in the basket and
climbed to the top
of the tree.

Hamish was so excited that
he fell on to the pie. Mrs Grinling
lowered the basket to the ground.

Mr Grinling was delighted to see Hamish home again.
"Just in time too," he said. "Please, Hamish, I need your help.
If Mrs Grinling cooks you another Star-gazy Pie could you
persuade the mice to find a new home?"
Hamish meowed.

Next morning Hamish and Mr Grinling
rowed out to the lighthouse.

While Mr Grinling worked, Hamish visited the mice.

When the Inspector of Lighthouses visited there were no mice scampering or squeaking. Mr Grinling was very happy. He patted Hamish fondly. "A great mouse chaser," he said.

The mice were very happy. They nibbled some crumbs and tried not to squeak.

HAMISH

Hamish was very happy. He stretched out beside the stove. "Well, my quivering ginger whiskers," he thought, "he's right about that. I'm the cleverest, I'm the greatest, I'm the lighthouse cat."